THE
LOST
SPHINX

MEGAN LINSKI & ALICIA RADES

CHAPTER ONE
GIANNA

I could hear it rattling in my ears, inescapable, unavoidable, harboring the call of death. *Thump. Thump. Thump.* I was certain it was the pounding of my own heart pummeling against my ribs for all to hear, betraying my concealment in the darkness as the royal guards pursued me. But as I peered down the village streets, terror tightened in my veins as I saw what those treacherous guards were really doing.

The gallows. The guards were constructing them in the town square, getting them ready for some poor soul to swing at the end of the noose come daybreak.

If I had anything to say about it, there would be no one for them to hang.

I snuck from one alleyway to another beneath the cover of night, knowing that if I were caught anywhere near the jail where they were holding my friend, I too would meet a dark fate at sunrise. I prayed to the gods for a vision to help me sneak past the guards, but no insight came. I had to work carefully, or Deryn and I would both perish before the kingdom itself collapsed.

The streets were normally empty at this time of night, but peasants traded whispers through doorways and armored guards hunted for any signs of traitors. Hoofbeats clomped against the cobblestone. I sank deeper into the shadows, pressing my back to the cool stone of a nearby building.

"This way!" a man shouted. A dozen guards galloped by without a glance toward the alleyway, riding black horses that rolled their heads, exposing the whites in their eyes.

I clutched the sword in my hand tighter as I peered onto the street. The guards were past me now, but I'd have to sneak into the town square where more were gathered in order to reach Deryn's holding cell.

I'd never had to use a sword before, as my position in the temple under the Oracle required knowledge rather than physical strength. But I'd been training with Deryn since we were children. I often won our sparring sessions, despite the fact that he had formal practice from the most decorated knights at the palace, and I merely had his guidance to go by.

It wasn't *proper* for a psychic sorceress to wield a sword, but Deryn had insisted that it wasn't right for a young woman like me to grow up unable to defend herself. If only the townsfolk knew that Gianna Fairbriar was getting swordplay lessons in secret from Prince Deryn himself. What a scandal that would be. My light footing made it easy to sneak up unnoticed, and my agile movements gave me an advantage over their strength. I couldn't hesitate to kill my opponent, and I wouldn't—not when Deryn's life was on the line.

I pulled the hood of my cloak over my red hair, then crossed the road silently. Purple and gold banners swayed in the wind overhead. They'd been hung to celebrate the coronation that was supposed to happen today — a coronation that had been delayed by an assassination attempt.

Five days ago, King Severin passed away. As was customary, a funeral was held at the temple, and subjects from all over the kingdom came to pay their respects. The monarchy moved quickly to crown Prince Alion, the eldest of the three princes, as to not leave a gap in leadership.

Then this morning the second eldest brother, Prince Helis, had stabbed Prince Alion with a dagger in his dressing chambers before the ceremony could begin. Word had traveled quickly through the streets of Mystic Peak. No one could believe what Helis had done. Alion and Helis were twin brothers, but Alion was three minutes older, which made him first in line for the throne. In a jealous rage, Helis had tried to kill his brother to gain the crown. When the guards caught him in the act, Helis fled.

I could hardly believe it myself. I liked Helis growing up, though I hadn't spent as much time with him as I had Deryn. I was the same age as Deryn, who was the youngest prince at just twenty-one years old. After the king's death, something dark awoke within Helis that I prayed I'd never have to witness again, and Deryn was in danger because of it.

I shot a glance over my shoulder. The peaks of the temple's spires towered high above the other buildings. I shuddered to think of what I'd watched happen there earlier tonight.

Rana— the great sphinx and Oracle of the realm, and my mentor— was taken from the temple by none other than Prince Helis. I tried to stop it, but Helis and his supporters had taken her before I could do anything.

Rana was a powerful being. With the body of a lion, the head of a woman, and mighty feathered wings, she had far greater strength than any human. She was the most powerful psychic in the realm, and her visions held great power. But a single sphinx was no match against twenty strong guards and their unbreakable iron chains.

Rana was a gifted prophet, and though I trusted her visions with my life, such power could not be summoned by will. I knew Helis had captured Rana to try and force her to foresee the future, so he could use her to defeat Alion and rule over all. I feared the Oracle's gift wouldn't be enough to save her from the vengeful prince and his guards.

I'd run from the temple immediately to alert the monarchy and seek aid. On my way to the palace, I heard the whispers. Prince Deryn had been arrested by Alion's men for allegedly aiding in the assassination attempt and helping Helis escape.

I knew better, and I didn't need a vision to prove it. Deryn was my closest friend. He would never harm one of his brothers, let alone go along with kidnapping Rana, who meant so much to me. Deryn was innocent, and Prince Alion was reacting irrationally because he was afraid that if one brother could try to kill him, there was nothing stopping the other from trying.

Prince Alion could use his fear for good to barricade the city and protect his people from Prince Helis' nefarious plans. Instead, he was allowing his guards to stomp through the street in the middle of the night while actively readying the gallows to take the life of his innocent younger brother.

I sympathized with Prince Alion, but he was going about this all wrong. Now that Rana was missing, his royal consultants would be further misguided.

I didn't need Prince Alion to stop this, though. Rana was the most valuable prophet in our nation. If I could find where Helis took her, I could free her, and her visions would calm this chaos before the kingdom shattered to pieces.

Rana wasn't strong enough to stop Helis' guards, which meant I needed a creature stronger to help me free her. *No one* was stronger than a dragon shifter. I had to rescue Deryn, not just because I cared for him deeply, but because the fate of the entire kingdom relied on it.

I crossed another street, creeping closer to the town square. Far past the square and up the mountain, a formidable castle stood overlooking the kingdom. I thought of all the times I'd been there, running through the corridors with Deryn or playing in the caves within the mountain. If we couldn't rescue Rana and prove Deryn's innocence, then I feared neither of us would ever return to the palace.

Deryn would find somewhere else to go, I was certain. He'd be devastated to lose his family, but perhaps he'd find a home among the dragon shifters. He was the only shifter in the city, and he'd once confessed to me his desire to leave royal life behind to find other dragon shifters like himself. It would be a long, arduous journey, as no one knew where to find the other dragon shifters— not even the Oracle.

Deryn wouldn't care what it took. He would leave the kingdom and travel across the realm if he had to. He just needed a starting point guiding him toward the drag-ons, and then he would be gone.

It ached my heart knowing that I couldn't convince him to stay. I always pictured a future with Deryn, and I couldn't imagine a life without him. It wasn't unusual for royals to marry spiritual leaders, and for a long time, I thought that's where we were headed. Then Deryn confessed to me his desire, but we never began a courtship. We couldn't, knowing it would never work between us. Deryn knew I couldn't leave Mystic Peak. I'd grown up in the temple, training with the Oracle. One day, I would become an Oracle myself. My entire life and my future were here, so I couldn't be a part of Deryn's journey, leaving the realm in search of the dragon shifters.

I wanted nothing but the best for him, so it didn't matter how I felt about him or what my intuition told me. It wouldn't work between us because he wished to leave Mystic Peak, and I had to stay.

I shook off any thoughts of a potential future with Deryn, because all that mattered right now was the task in front of me. If I didn't pull this off, there wouldn't *be* a future for either of us— together or apart.

The town's jail was situated two streets over from the square. This road was relatively void of guards, but every now and then a group of them would come hurtling through on horseback. From here, the sounds of the gallows being constructed and the shouts of men only grew louder. I could see through gaps between the buildings that the square was full of weapons, including crossbows, longbows, and sharp swords. They even had a catapult, as if to scare off anyone who might protest Deryn's execution. I knew one wrong move would do me in.

I crept around the building toward the only entrance. Two guards stood on either side of the front door. The jail was rather benign, with stone walls and the smallest of barred windows high above the guards' heads. It wasn't a large structure, as long-term criminals were kept in the dungeons at the palace where the monarchy could keep a close eye on them. These cells in town were specifically reserved for those criminals awaiting execution.

I crouched in the shadows to assess the guards for weak points. These guards wore armor from head to toe, with heavy metal helmets and strong breastplates. The only way to get past them was a sure aim of my sword between the joints where one piece of armor met another— and I had to do it before they got a swing in of their own, because I had no armor to protect myself. I thanked the stars there were only two of them, but I couldn't take them both on at once.

I listened for the sounds of incoming soldiers, but I

heard none. Lifting a rock I found at my feet, I tossed it as far as I could near the next alleyway.

The guards heard the clatter, and their hands immediately went to the swords on their hips.

"What was that?" one of them demanded.

"Someone's lurking nearby." The second guard sounded certain. "I'll go check it out."

The second guard approached the abandoned alleyway I'd thrown the rock toward. That's when I sprang from the shadows, coming at the first guard from the side. He caught sight of me and lifted his sword, but I'd already anticipated his reaction, and I was faster than he was. The tip of my sword jabbed upward, straight into the narrow gap beneath his breastplate.

The man gave a pained grunt, and blood spurted from his abdomen and onto the street. I yanked my blade from his flesh before his knees hit the ground. His armor clanked against the cobblestone from behind me as I raced toward the second guard.

The guard had heard the commotion and came running back, but I was already swinging my sword when he sprinted out of the alleyway. My heavy weapon clanged against his helmet, sending it flying off his head. He swung at me, but I ducked out of the way and rolled across the ground. His sword connected with the street merely an inch from where I'd landed. Perhaps the stars had heard my prayers after all.

In one swift motion, I sprang back to my feet and used all my strength to swing my sword at the exposed skin on his neck. My blade cut through the delicate flesh there, and he gave a gurgle as he fell to the ground.

I didn't have time to feel remorse. I grabbed the keyring that hung off the guard's belt, then turned toward the jail and barged through the front doors.

In the cell at the end stood a lone figure, his hands wrapped around the bars and a startled look on his face. My heart swelled at the sight of Prince Deryn's hazel eyes and the familiar dark curls that fell across his face. His features softened when I yanked back my hood.

"Gianna." Deryn's voice sounded like a song. "What are you doing here? If you're caught, you'll be killed!"

I marched up to his cell, my sword still dripping with blood. "I know you're innocent, Deryn. I'm here to break you out."

CHAPTER TWO
DERYN

I had never experienced devastation like when the royal guard stormed into my quarters and mercilessly dragged me to this jail cell without the dignity of a trial. One moment, I was a well-respected prince, and the next, I was being sentenced to death for Helis' crimes, in which I played no part.

I had been here for hours and unable to summon my strength, as the bars I stood behind had been enchanted to suppress any magical abilities. I couldn't shift into my dragon form, nor summon any fire. All I could do was listen to the sound of the guards constructing the gallows.

I desperately feared for my life, not just because the gallows were imminent, but because tight spaces like this cell terrified me. I'd been afraid of small places since I was a child, since my brothers used to leave me alone inside the tight crevices within the Cryptic Caves. I thought we'd gone to the caves to play, but was laughed at when I couldn't get out.

Dragons weren't meant to be caged. We were born to spread our wings, though my brothers would know nothing of that. I didn't inherit my dragon shifting powers, but was gifted them by the gods when I was a child, long before I could remember. I'd been born sick and dying, and when my parents prayed to the stars to heal me, the god of the dragon shifters came down from the skies to give me strength. Through this power, I developed the ability to become a dragon myself.

There were other dragon shifters out there, though I didn't know where to find them. In my heart of hearts, I knew I belonged with them.

I loved my brothers dearly, but I never truly fit in among the humans. I believed I was always meant to become a dragon. As was customary when children in the kingdom were born, the Oracle Rana had imparted a gift of wisdom on me. I knew her blessing by heart: *An inferno can spark from the smallest ember.*

Even the sphinx knew upon my birth what I was destined for. But my destiny couldn't be fulfilled here in Mystic Peak. I was a prince, but as the youngest prince, I held no true rank and was of no use to these people. I belonged among the dragon shifters.

That's why I was packing my bags before the coronation. Before he died, my father had promised to help me find the dragon city. Now that he was gone I would have to discover them myself. I had planned to stay for my brother's coronation ceremony, and then I would begin my journey to find others like me.

Prince Alion took my packed bags as a sign of guilt once Helis tried to kill him. That's when the guards arrested me for an assassination attempt I had no knowledge of.

Alion would make a great king, and I trusted he knew what was best for the realm, but this imprisonment brought me back to those days of teasing in the Cryptic Caves— only this time, it wasn't a joke. I never imagined he would lock me up like this, but Alion had jumped to conclusions, and I would be the one to pay for the oversight. My only hope of survival was to plot a well-timed escape that I'd have to pull off somewhere between here and the gallows. But I knew my brother possessed enchanted shackles, and I wasn't sure I'd manage to survive them once they took me out of this cell and put a noose around my neck. I thought for certain all was lost.

Now Gianna had stormed into the jail, and a familiar fire ignited within my stomach in her presence. *Hope.* I saw that she clutched tightly to the sword I'd gifted her. The years we'd spent training had paid off.

She sheathed her sword, and I reached through the bars to take her hands in mine. I had to feel the warmth of her skin to prove to myself she was truly here. I wouldn't believe this wasn't some trick of sorcery otherwise. I was sure I'd gone completely mad, until I felt her solid and cool hands against mine. Her touch always calmed me.

I smoothed down her red strands of hair. "How did you know where to find me?"

"News of the assassination attempt spread quickly across the kingdom," Gianna explained. "Everyone thinks you plotted the assassination with Helis."

"I knew nothing of Helis' plans."

"I know that, but as long as Prince Alion suspects your involvement, the kingdom will be calling for your head. Prince Alion wasn't crowned king today, but his word still reigns supreme. He's not going to consider a trial as long as Helis is still out there."

"What Helis did was wrong, but there must be some part of Alion that believes I had nothing to do with it."

Gianna shook her head firmly. "You don't understand. I figured Helis would be long gone after the assassination attempt this morning, but he came back for Rana. There's only one reason he would want her— to force visions out of her so he can overthrow Alion for good."

This was worse than I thought. "Shouldn't Rana have seen this coming?"

"It's the Oracle's job to protect the realm, and mine

as well, but neither Rana nor I received any insight about this. She's more powerful than I am, but I'm certain if she'd received a vision about any of this, she'd have tried to stop it. We are only privy to the information and visions the gods wish to share."

"When was she taken?"

"Shortly before sundown. I witnessed it myself. Helis and his loyalists stormed the temple and shackled Rana."

"You're sure it was him?" I still had a hard time believing Helis could do this, and that someone in the kingdom hadn't disguised themselves to take upon his image, magically or otherwise.

"I know your brother's face."

"My brothers are twins. Helis has a birthmark shaped like the sun on his shoulder. Alion's is the moon," I reminded her. "Did you see Helis' birthmark?"

Their marks tied into the wisdom the sphinx imparted on them at birth: *The moon comes before the sun.* Their life wisdom indicated Alion as the eldest and first in line for the throne. If there was no birthmark, then that meant this had to be an imposter that assumed my brother's identity.

"Helis has light eyes, similar to the sun, and Alion has dark eyes like the night. I saw his eyes, and they were definitely light, not to mention Helis was wearing his cloak with the suns embroidered on it when he captured

Rana. I've seen him wear it a hundred times. That's how I know it was him."

My stomach dropped. "So it *was* Helis. Damn him."

"Deryn, you're always trying to see the best in people even when they only want to show you the worst. I know you don't want to believe that Helis could betray both of you like this, but he did. He tried to kill Alion because he wanted the throne, and he let you take the fall for it. I'm sorry, but you have to accept he wasn't the person you thought he was."

Gianna was right. I loved Helis, but he had always been a bit of an odd character, always creeping around the palace and sneaking off royal grounds, hiding strange secrets he didn't want to tell me about. Not to mention he'd always bullied me growing up. Both of my brothers did, but maybe Helis had truly meant the teasing. I'd tried to see him in a good light, but I'd misjudged his character. "You're right, Gia. He's been plotting this all along. So what was Helis doing when you were there?"

"He was ruthless, screaming at a guard for merely bumping into him. I saw all the signs of a man enraged enough with power to kill his own brother. I regret that I couldn't stop it."

Tears welled in her eyes, and I stroked her cheek. "You don't have to do this alone, Gianna."

She sniffled. "We have to find her, Deryn."

"Let's move quickly. We must get out of here before the guards discover us."

Gianna shoved the proper key into the lock on my cell door. The metal clanged as the door swung open, and I breathed a sigh of relief as I swept her up in my arms. She squeezed me back in a tight embrace.

I drew away. "Have you had any visions of where Helis might be?"

She shook her head. "It doesn't work that way. Sometimes I can gain insight by having something physical to trigger a vision, but otherwise, I can't control what comes to me. I need something that's close to Helis to use as a starting point, an object of his that I can use to pull magic from."

"We could go to his quarters," I suggested.

"The palace is too heavily guarded. We'll never get in. We need something unprotected I can touch, and I don't know if there's anything that has a strong enough connection to him to get a vision."

Something struck me. "What about the Pool of Kenory?"

The magical pool held the memories of all the realm. Individuals from across the kingdom traveled there to place their memories into the water.

"The Pool doesn't give up memories, not even to the Oracle," Gianna countered. "It's not a place of visions."

"But it was important to Helis," I emphasized. "He

used to sneak out of his chambers at night to go there, though he swore me to secrecy when I discovered he was sneaking around."

Gianna's features fell. "Do you think he could've been planning this assassination for a while? He must've gone to the Pool of Kenory for years trying to get information, so he could come up with a plan to overthrow Alion at the right time."

"I'm not sure how long he was planning this, but it's clear that he was using the Pool to try and gain power," I admitted. "Regardless, he has a connection to the Pool of Kenory. We might be able to use it to trigger your visions and guide us to wherever he's taken Rana."

"Then let's get moving."

We ran to the doors, but skidded to a halt when we came onto the street surrounded by twenty guards. Directly in front of us, General Skyglade aimed a crossbow in our direction. He'd been my father's most trusted military leader and had taught me combat one-on-one since I was a young child. It didn't seem sane how quickly he could turn on me just because Alion gave the order to kill me.

"Halt!" General Skyglade's voice echoed through the village.

Gianna and I didn't have a moment to pause.

"On my back," I hissed at her, and I was shifting before the guards could react. My limbs elongated twice my height in an instant, and my clothes disappeared to be replaced by strong, shimmering scales the color of obsidian. Wings that spanned the length of three buildings sprouted from my back, and a long, hooked tail appeared on my backside. Guards were shoved aside as my impressive dragon form took up most of the street.

Without wasting a moment, Gianna reached up to grab hold of one of my spines, then swung herself onto my back. Guards sprinted forward to swing their swords at my face, but I opened my mouth to let out a roar that reverberated all the way to the peak of the mountain and back. Fire erupted from my throat, and the guards scrambled back.

I spread my wings and kicked off the cobblestone. General Skyglade shouted obscenities as he pulled the trigger on his crossbow. The arrow struck me in the side and shattered upon impact. It hurt, but it was unable to penetrate my iron-hard scales.

"Ready the catapult!" General Skyglade shouted.

Gianna's legs tightened around me. "Faster!"

An arrow wouldn't hurt me, but a catapult would knock me out of the sky. I pumped my wings harder than I ever had before, desperately fighting the winds to gain height. The royal guard already wanted my head, but they weren't taking Gianna down with me.

I heard the sound of the catapult deploying, and I

dipped lower to avoid its aim. The projectile flew over-head, but I continued spiraling downward.

Gianna screamed as we plummeted in a freefall. "What are you doing!?"

"I'm getting us out of here alive," I told her.

As I dipped toward the town square, heat billowed upward in my throat. Fire erupted from my mouth, consuming the catapults and the gallows all in one blow. Guards scrambled every which way trying to put out the flames.

I didn't wish to take out the village completely or to harm any bystanders, so I left it at that. I turned my gaze upward and climbed high in the sky until Gianna and I were concealed by the clouds.

General Skyglade's words echoed from below me. "Mark my words, Prince Deryn. You will perish with the rest of them!"

The general wanted me to be taken down with Helis, but I wasn't going to let that happen. We'd go to the Pool of Kenory, find where Helis had taken Rana, then rescue the sphinx and bring order back to Mystic Peak.

I could only pray the kingdom wasn't already doomed.

CHAPTER THREE
GIANNA

It was close to dawn when I'd broken Deryn out, and the sun was rising over the mountains. The skies were flecked with orange, red and gold, and I nearly wept at the beauty of the gorgeous dawn as it crested over the peaks. Deryn let out a soft *hmph,* emitting smoke from his nose. I reached down to gently pet his shoulder, drawing my fingers across his scales.

We'd experienced so many sunrises just like this together. Treasured moments I tucked away for safe keeping in my heart, morning flights that always took my breath away.

But I needed to realize this wasn't permanent. It wasn't like I'd get to wake up next to Deryn every day like I wanted to. We couldn't be together. We both knew that, though my heart desperately told me that wasn't true. We'd save the sphinx, then once we got Rana back,

Deryn and I would go our separate ways. This was temporary. We'd already said goodbye to each other once before, and we needed to keep that promise to prevent ourselves from hurting each other more than we already had.

Deryn snorted. *"Gianna. You've been avoiding me for weeks. We should talk about... us."*

"There's nothing to talk about."

"That's not fair. You're the one who ended our courtship. You haven't spoken to me since."

"Because I've already made up my mind. I'm not leaving with you to find the dragon shifters. My place is in Mystic Peak."

"We could make it work somehow. It doesn't have to be the end for us, Gia."

My chest tightened, feeling like my heart was breaking in two. "We have different paths, different lives. I'm going to become an Oracle, and you're going to go off on an adventure to find your kind. Those two dreams can't both come true. One of us will have to sacrifice what they want, and that's not fair to either of us."

"We can find a way."

Tears burned at the corners of my eyes as I whispered, "Please stop, Deryn. It hurts me to keep going over this. Just let it be."

He fell silent, not wanting to wound me further. It

was probably for the best. We'd had this conversation a hundred times. We wouldn't find another solution even if we talked about it a hundred times more. Might as well focus on the mission.

"The Pool's here. I'm taking us down." Deryn redirected his flight, and we landed in a circular clearing that was lush with long green grass, towering trees and hordes of butterflies.

I slid off his back and he transformed, reaching for my hand. "Gianna."

I pulled my fingers out of his sharply. "Not now, Deryn."

I wouldn't let him convince me to fall into those hazel eyes again. Not this time.

We approached a silvery pond that shimmered like sapphires. I could hear whispers as we drew near; the memories of all who came to swim in the Pool of Kenory, and share their knowledge with the timeless waters. Deryn said Helis had bathed here multiple times. He must've left some of his knowledge behind as a result.

"If I touch the Pool, I might be able to get a vision about where Helis went," I suggested. "Watch my back?"

Deryn nodded. I approached the Pool, kneeling at the side of the water. Before I could skim the surface, a ferocious snarl emitted from the tall reeds surrounding the pool.

Deryn snatched my wrist and yanked me backward as a creature leapt from the opposite bank, sailing over the water and landing before us on four paws. My insides rattled with fear as I witnessed a lion the size of a small dragon with a scorpion's tail and black bat wings prowl the edge of the pool. A manticore— one of the deadliest beasts in the realm.

The manticore sprung, but Deryn pushed me out of the way and transformed. He jumped at the manticore, burying his fangs in the monster's mane. The manticore snarled and used his sharp claws to bat at Deryn's face, digging his claws in, although the nails couldn't puncture scales. The earth thundered as the dragon and manticore rolled around, snarling in a mess of teeth and fangs.

I ripped my sword out of its hilt and charged with a yell, taking a swing toward the manticore's poisonous tail. The manticore hissed and whipped his tail out of the way, letting go of Deryn and backing off. "*Do not seek to take my poison from me, human, unless you wish to die. You have intruded upon my home, and I must defend it.*"

I lowered my sword slightly. "We don't want to bother you. We only wish to use the Pool."

"*Only one who proves themselves worthy may caress its waters,*" the manticore snapped. "*You have proven yourself in battle, but can you prove the strength of your mind?"*

"Enough," Deryn growled, transforming back into a man and planting himself between me and the beast. "We didn't come here to fight you. We came to use the Pool, so we can figure out where my brother is."

"Who may this brother be, and why is it so important to find him?" the manticore asked.

"Prince Helis. He has committed crimes against the kingdom, and must be stopped. He kidnapped the Oracle and fled the area, but it is imperative we bring him to justice."

The manticore paused. *"Helis kidnapped the sphinx? I am surprised he would go to such lengths to achieve his goals, but I suppose the Oracle has knowledge even the Pool cannot give him."*

"He spoke to you about his plans to take over the kingdom?" I questioned.

"Not at length, although he often complained that his elder brother, Alion, would be an unfit ruler once Severin died, and that someone else should take the job. I was unaware he wanted it to be himself." The manticore sat on his haunches. *"I am called Grimfang. I have been the guardian of this Pool since the beginning of time, and I will be here long after everyone in this world is gone, guarding this Pool still."*

"You won't be if you don't help us," Deryn threatened.

"Deryn! That's not helping," I snapped.

Against my better judgement, I came closer to Grimfang. "Please. If the Oracle remains missing, the entire realm will fall. We need your help to put a stop to Helis' plans, and bring her home."

Grimfang blinked. *"Helis was my friend. I do not get many visitors who return to the Pool of Kenory, but Helis swam within its waters often. We spoke of philosophy each time he visited for hours. I do not wish to betray him."*

"Then don't," I said. "Just let the Pool show us what it wants us to see."

Grimfang sighed. *"I will not help you defeat Helis, as I consider him a dear ally. But I do not agree with his plan to conquer the kingdom. I will not stop you from going after him, but if you wish to gain access to the Pool, you must first prove your knowledge by passing my riddle, and offering up a piece of wisdom. No one who may swim within the Pool can access it without proving their intelligence, and giving something that the Pool may keep for all eternity."*

"What's the riddle?" Deryn asked.

Grimfang closed his eyes and hummed. *"How may one foresee the past, and yet remember the future?"*

"That doesn't make any sense. The past has already happened and the future hasn't taken place yet," Deryn argued, but I held up a hand to think it over.

Long moments passed, until a piece of wisdom Rana had once bestowed upon me surfaced to mind.

"History," I replied. "History repeats itself. The only way to *remember* the future is to foresee what has already happened in the past. Learning from your mistakes is the only way you can avoid what's coming, and make change before the cycle repeats itself."

"*Correct,*" Grimfang said. "*You have passed the second test. Now, what knowledge may you offer the Pool to keep in exchange for its wisdom?*"

I wasn't sure, but Deryn stepped forward. "I will give you the name of the dragon god who blessed me with my powers. No one else in the kingdom knows it, but I do. The god's name is Solfyre. Even as a newborn, the magic caused the name to be imprinted upon my heart. It's the first memory I ever had."

He'd never told me about that. It must've been something he kept secret from everyone. Grimfang nodded. "*Very well. Both of you, place your hands into the Pool. The dragon shifter, to give up his wisdom, and the psychic, to take whatever knowledge the Pool may give her.*"

Grimfang let us pass. We knelt beside the Pool, and I

swallowed nervously before I went to dip my hand in. At the last second, Deryn grasped my hand in his, and both of us plunged our fingers into the Pool together. A vision hit me immediately, images coming at me from all sides.

I wandered outside the palace grounds, circling the stone towers. I came to a bush blooming with a variety of yellow flowers and moved the thorny branches aside.

Behind the thorns was a door, covered with vines and barely standing. I opened the door, moving through dark hallways, winding avenues. I came to another door, this one iron in make. As I opened it, I entered into a small room where only a few candles burned, providing little light. I turned in place, observing forbidden books, stacks of scrolls, and maps... dozens upon dozens of maps.

It was only then I realized I was seeing the world through Helis' eyes as he experienced a memory... a very recent memory.

The vision abruptly ended, sealing me off from anything further. I came out of the vision slowly, shaking my head. "Helis has a hideout. A secret passage in the castle where he keeps all his hidden scrolls. If he has any information on where he took the Oracle, it'll be there."

"Then let's go." Deryn changed again, and I grabbed a spike to haul myself upon his back. I cursed myself for the shivers that raced down my spine when I touched him, trying to focus on saving the Oracle and not pleasing my heart.

"Take caution," Grimfang warned as we wandered out of the clearing. *"Helis is craftier than you give him credit for. To defeat him, you must also be."*

CHAPTER FOUR
DERYN

The entire town was looking for us when we returned to Mystic Peak. I could hear soldiers running around even from a distance, demanding to be told where Gianna Fairbriar and Prince Deryn had hidden themselves. I landed in the nearby woods outside of town and transformed back into a man so we could sneak in. Everyone would notice a dragon coming, and we needed to remain elusive. Once we got into town, we kept our hoods up and remained concealed in the bustling city streets, hiding within the safety of crowds until we got to the boundaries of the royal palace.

I'd roamed these grounds freely only a few days before, and now I was a wanted man. How things changed. I knew Alion would kill me on sight if he saw me, and he wouldn't hesitate to harm Gianna, either. I'd die before I let anything happen to her. We had to get into that hideout, find out what Helis was concealing, and leave before we were caught.

Most of the guards were at the barracks at this time of day, practicing combat and marching formations, and the rest of Alion's men had been sent into Mystic Peak to look for us after we'd escaped last night. We only had a short window of time to get in and out. We came to the stone wall that surrounded the castle, and I boosted Gianna onto my back. Using my dragon strength, I climbed up the twelve-foot wall and vaulted myself over the edge, landing on my feet. We'd landed in the gardens, which were deserted, but it would only take one servant to walk by for an alert to be sounded.

Gianna slid off my back, and I took her hand in mine to pull her behind me as we ran through the flowers. We'd done this so many times, but now, our path was deadly and urgent. Didn't stop me from enjoying the feel of her skin against mine as we approached the bush with the yellow flowers, the one Gianna had spoken of in her vision.

I found the door and wrenched it open. Once we were in the dark passageway, I used my dragon magic to light a fireball in my hand for light.

Gianna led the way, navigating the winding hall-ways until we came to a thick iron door. "Here."

It was locked, but that wasn't a problem for me. I

used my dragon strength to bash the lock apart. The door swung open, hanging off its hinges. I found myself growing hollow as I observed the piles of papers, the mountains of books and the copious amounts of records. *Huh, Helis. I didn't know you were keeping this much from me.*

And I'd thought we'd been so close. I was a fool.

"Start searching," Gianna said, already browsing through stacks of parchment. "Wherever he took the Oracle, I'm sure these scrolls can tell us."

I used the fireball to light the candles in the room, then allowed it to fizzle out as I started churning through papers. There was so much here, and we didn't know what we were looking for. It could take days to go through all of this, but we only had hours before we were discovered, if that.

But I trusted Gianna's magic, and what was more, I trusted Gianna. I'd put my life in that woman's hands without a second thought any time she asked me to. Her vision would lead us somewhere, I was sure.

"Anything yet?" I asked impatiently after fifteen minutes of searching. All I'd located were a bunch of dusty history books, which weren't getting us anywhere.

"I found a whole archive about Queen Kosara inside his desk," Gianna said reluctantly. "Sorry, Deryn. It seems like Helis was obsessed with preserving her memory."

I said nothing. My mother had died many years ago during a bandit attack. It had happened as she was traveling through the Alype Mountains to visit her sister. I'd barely been a toddler at the time, so I could hardly remember her, though I secretly believed my brothers blamed me for her death. She was visiting my aunt to use her extensive library, to research where the dragons could be hiding. She never would've made the trip otherwise.

Just more blood on my hands that I would eventually have to atone for. No wonder Helis had framed me and Alion had sentenced me to death. Both of them wanted revenge against me for killing our mother, though they'd gone about it in different ways.

I wasn't a part of this family, not really, and never would be. I should've left years ago to find the dragons like I wanted, but... Gianna. She was the only reason I stayed. She was the only piece of Mystic Peak worth keeping, and I wanted her all to myself, though she was determined to ward me away and run me off.

I wouldn't give up on us. Not until I was sure she didn't want this, and her hand lingering on my scales for longer than it should've earlier told me she still loved me. We'd find the Oracle, then I'd convince her we could continue our courtship and have a life together.

Or she'd tell me to leave, and I'd finally go. Besides finding the other dragons, the only thing I wanted to do in this life was make her happy. If that meant my absence, so be it. Even if it ripped me in two to part from her.

"I don't understand why he's keeping all these records. Some of this stuff is centuries old." Gianna coughed as she blew dust off a scroll.

"He's been studying, trying to conceive a master plan. He wants to make himself into this great historical figure who will be talked about for ages, so he's been keeping all these records to get inspiration for his rule. He must've been plotting this for a long time."

Gianna paused. "Do you think he had something to do with King Severin's death?"

I wasn't sure. My father had died in pain, gasping for breath with welts all over his body. It sure seemed like someone had poisoned him, and after what I'd found, I wouldn't put it past Helis to do it.

"If he did kill my father, we'll bring him to justice." I opened another book, hoping to find a clue inside. Helis had bookmarked this page. It detailed the laws for a line of succession for the kingdom; that if a king died, the realm passed down to his eldest child, unless that child was seen unfit to rule. Then it went to the next sibling in line.

Helis had circled the page in ink, his cursive handwriting scrawling out the words, *This is the way.*

If that wasn't incriminating. Gianna read over my

shoulder. "So that's it. He's trying to prove Alion isn't fit to rule so he can take the throne for himself."

I turned the page. Tucked into the book was a folded piece of paper. I unfolded it, and saw that it was a map of the realm and the surrounding wilderness. On the map was a spot marked miles outside of Mystic Peak. Helix's handwriting was inscribed by the marker. *Here is the best spot.*

"The ink is still bright and fresh. He wrote this recently." I pointed at the spot on the map. "I bet this is where he took the sphinx."

Gianna's eyes narrowed as she observed the region I was gesturing to. "The Shadowed Range. It *would* be a good place to keep the Oracle. No one lives out there. It's practically abandoned."

"Exactly." I rolled up the map and pocketed it. "Let's follow the map to the location marked. The Oracle *has* to be there."

We extinguished the candles and left the room. We'd need to preserve the hideout for evidence once we brought Helis in. I poked my head out the door once we got to the end of the hidden corridor, and saw that the gardens were now completely swarming with guards. Combat practice had to be over, and now Alion's men were combing the area looking for intruders.

I bet they'd found our footprints. I cursed quietly

under my breath, but Gianna whispered, "I have an idea."

She eyed the horse stables, which weren't too far away. She went to head toward them, but I held her back. "Gianna, no. It's not safe. Let me do it."

"You're too tall. You'll get caught. I'm small, so no one will notice me. Just trust me."

Her beautiful eyes were so pleading. They pulled me in and made me agree, though I didn't want to. "Fine. But *be careful.*"

She nodded, then snuck off toward the stables. I held my breath, thinking she was going to be seen, but Gianna crouched behind pillars and statues in the gardens to remain concealed.

Once she ducked inside the stables, I felt my chest tighten in fear. I didn't like having her out of my sight, especially not now. Anything could happen to me and I'd accept my fate, but I'd perish a long and painful death before I allowed a single ill thing to befall her.

A breath came whooshing out of me as I watched an entire herd of horses come galloping out of the stables, cantering toward the guards. The stampede raced past the soldiers. The entire battalion began running after them, trying to catch the loose horses as they charged out of the gardens and to the front of the palace.

Gianna reappeared at my side a few moments later. "See? I had it handled."

I wanted to kiss her right there, but forced myself not to. "Impressive. Where'd you learn to be so stealthy?"

"*You* taught me that." She gave me a wayward smile that made my heart stutter. "Your prey can't see you coming if you stick to the shadows."

I wrapped an arm around her shoulders to guide her as we hurried back toward the palace wall. "Let's just make sure Helis doesn't see *us* coming. We don't know what's waiting for us once we get where we're going, and we could have a fight on our hands."

"Then let him fight us. As long as we're together— I mean, *working together*— he can't beat us," Gianna replied confidently.

My spirit flew at the slightest slip of her tongue, but I couldn't get my hopes up too high. We didn't know what Helis was doing to the Oracle right now, and if we were too late to save her, Gianna would be devastated. I knew what the Oracle meant to her.

As a child, Gianna had been orphaned and abandoned on the streets. She'd nearly died in poverty and suffering before Rana had found her, and taken her in. The Oracle was more like a mother to Gianna than a mentor. As such, she'd never get over allowing Helis to hurt Rana if something bad had taken place.

And I wouldn't be able to comfort her if that happened, no matter how much I cared. So I vowed to myself that neither Gianna nor the Oracle would get hurt. Even if that meant putting my life on the line.

CHAPTER FIVE
GIANNA

As we flew toward the mountains at the furthest edges of the kingdom, the clouds darkened, and the terrain became shadowed with the threat of a great storm brewing overhead. There was a reason this place was called the Shadowed Range; the barren mountains were under a constant cover of gloom. It was strange, because as much as it seemed to rain here, there were no plants, just steep, jagged mountain peaks as far as the eye could see. It appeared as if it must be a cursed land.

These mountains stood outside the borders of the kingdom, as neither King Severin nor the monarchs who came before him ever bothered to claim the area. There was nothing here worth having, and even if there were precious metals or gems hidden within these rocks, anyone who tried to get to them would die along the treacherous journey.

The mountains rose so high they seemed to scrape the sky, and the cliffsides were so steep that making passage would require travelers to climb hand over foot the entire way. Boulders could fall unexpectedly at any moment, and the unsteady rock could send any explorer tumbling into crevices they'd never escape. Whatever Prince Helis was hiding here was certainly well concealed.

"The map indicates that Helis is hiding just beyond the tallest mountain." I pointed ahead.

We were so close to finding Helis. I could feel it in my bones. When we did, I was making him give Rana back to me. She'd saved me from the streets as a child, and I still owed her so much. I wasn't going home without her.

"*Hang on tight,*" Deryn told me.

I tightened my grip on his spines as Deryn soared over the tallest mountain. As we came to the other side of it, he dipped downward. We broke out of the clouds, and my jaw dropped in amazement as an oasis appeared below.

Tucked deep within the mountain range, beyond where anyone had ventured before, was a beautiful valley that took my breath away. Greenery crept up the sides of the cliffs, and waterfalls cascaded out of caves and into a river below. The blue water shimmered as if it was enchanted.

Deryn flew down into the valley to get out of the fog. Tall cliffs rose on either side of us, and he had to twist from one side to the other to follow the winding river through the canyon. Yet as we rounded a bend, my heart dropped.

Before us, the beauty of the valley we witnessed moments ago seemed like a dream. Charred remains of what looked like a once thriving city appeared before us. Smoke still billowed into the air, which meant whatever happened here occurred recently. I choked back my breath to keep from inhaling the strong scent of scorched debris.

Deryn slowly descended, looking one way and then the other as he tried to take it all in. I couldn't make sense of it myself.

One half of the city looked to be built within the mountain itself, with homes carved out into the cliff-sides, while the other half was constructed with tradi-tional materials at the base of the canyon and along the river. All the homes made of wood were now ash, with nothing more than stone foundations to mark where they once stood. The buildings carved into the mountainside had crumbled to pieces, marked only by a few remaining archways that used to be windows.

Deryn's heavy feet landed against the stone street. I

slid off his back, but neither of us spoke as we took in the devastation.

Deryn shifted back into human form, and rubble crunched beneath our feet as we started forward. Shattered glass littered every walkway, and the remnants of iron chandeliers and stone fireplaces were all that remained of the crumbled homes. Cast iron cauldrons lay in heaps among metal bed frames and toppled stone archways. The architecture must've been impeccable before the city was destroyed, evidenced in shattered stained-glass windows that had maintained some of their vibrant color, though they were now covered in soot.

We continued down the dilapidated street. Deryn kicked aside debris, revealing a fine piece of porcelain that had been shattered but not burned. He picked it up and turned it around in his hands. Whomever it belonged to likely cherished it dearly. It appeared as if the city's residents once lived a lavish, abundant life here within the canyon.

I hoped to hear the voices of survivors, but the canyon was eerily silent. Not even the squawk of a bird reached our ears. I didn't see any bodies, but I sensed death with every step. The townsfolk had either perished completely in the flames, or their bodies remained trapped beneath the debris.

I tore my gaze away from the horrid scene. "This

town is completely deserted. If Helis brought Rana here, then she's already dead with the rest of them."

A small figurine within the rubble caught my eye, and I knelt to inspect it. It was shaped like a dragon and made of metal, so it hadn't burned in the fires. It appeared to be a children's toy. Gingerly, I reached out to touch it.

The heartbreak of our discovery was written in Deryn's voice. "What is this place? I've never heard of any settlement existing in the Shadowed Range."

I didn't answer, because I'd already touched the figurine. I barely heard Deryn as the sound of dying screams filled my ears. The frightened cries were deafening and felt like an arrow straight through my heart. Deryn couldn't hear them, but the screams were real all the same. They were *memories*, insight the gods had granted me to give context to what happened here.

I glanced upward. The rising spire of a single remaining building knocked the wind out of me. It was a temple, charred and broken, but refusing to crumble completely. A bell hung twisted at the top of the tower. That's when recognition hit me.

Deryn didn't know what this place was, but I knew *exactly* where we were, because I'd seen it in a vision before. It hadn't made any sense then, but now, I understood.

Slowly I rose to my feet, my voice turning hollow. "Deryn, this is the home of the lost dragon shifters."

CHAPTER SIX
DERYN

I struggled to understand what Gianna was saying. Doubt rose up, along with defiance. *No.* This couldn't be true. This barren place... it *couldn't* be the home of the dragon shifters, the people I'd been searching for all my life.

This wasn't much of a home. It was burnt to a crisp.

"How... how do you know?" I hardly managed to speak, but strangled out a few words besides..

Gianna turned her back, then whispered, "Follow me."

She led me away from the village. I wordlessly followed. She took me into a glen of trees that was thankfully far away from the destruction of the village and all its carnage. She sat on a broad rock beside a small creek, watching the water slowly trickle by.

I sat beside her. "You act like you know this place."

"I do, but I've never been here. I saw it before in a vision, but I didn't understand what it meant until now."

Gianna took a shuddering breath. "When the sphinx was taken, I tried to stop Helis. I was in the hallway of the temple, watching them capture her. I was concealed behind a wall, so Helis and his men didn't realize I was there. They didn't know I watched him take her. But I *couldn't* help her, because a vision overpowered me the moment I took a step to save her. When I received the vision, I collapsed, and I was trapped in that vision for gods know how long. When I woke up, Helis and the Oracle were gone, but I was left alone in the temple. Helis never saw me. That's the only reason I was able to get away and find you."

"Gia. What did your vision show you?"

A tear ran down Gianna's face as she gasped, "Destruction. Death. The annihilation of an entire race."

I said nothing, because I felt so endlessly cold. Gianna went on, her voice wrecked with grief. "The vision showed me soldiers storming into the dragon village at night. They killed everyone in their sleep, then burned the village to the ground. The dragons tried to fight back, but most of them were killed before they even got the chance to shift, and the ones that managed to transform died in the attempt to save their families. The bodies and all the buildings were turned to ash. I knew from the moment I came out of that vision that all the dragon shifters, and their home, had been destroyed."

My hopes, dreams, everything I had ever wanted, vanished into smoke. The one thing I'd desperately prayed for all my life had been torn away from me. My people— the dragon shifters— were dead. They'd had a village, and I'd found it, but I'd been too late to protect them. The gift the dragon god had given was wasted on me, because I hadn't gotten here in time to stop it.

"I wanted to tell you, but I just... couldn't. I couldn't bear the thought of crushing your dream." She sobbed, struggling to breathe. "I couldn't take that from you. At least not now. We've been trying to find the Oracle from the moment I had that vision, and every time I wanted to confess what I saw, I lost my voice. I knew how it would devastate you to learn that your kind was gone. I promised myself I'd tell you the truth once we rescued the Oracle, but she's not here. Now I think Helis killed her, too, along with all the dragons. Why else did he mark this place on the map unless he exterminated all these people? Why else would he want to kill all the dragon shifters unless he was worried about them interfering with his rule? Helis ordered his followers to come here before he attacked Alion, and they killed all the dragons. And from what I saw in my vision, I don't think any of them made it out alive."

I didn't believe that. I couldn't. Something in me

screamed that there had to be other dragon shifters out there... though the evidence around me insisted that hope was just a silly dream. Helis had killed them all. I needed to accept that instead of lying to myself.

I could barely think as I stared at her gorgeous, tearstained face. "But... you *knew* the dragon shifters were all dead. If you had told me, I would've given up on trying to find them, so I could stay with you in Mystic Peak."

"I'd never take anything from you, Deryn. Not even if it was to gain something I desperately wanted." Gianna wiped at her eyes. "Yes, I wanted you to stay with me. But I wanted you to be happy far more. So I knew I had to let you fly free. Or at least, let you hold onto the hope you could find others out there that were like you for at least a little while longer. I never want to cause you pain. If I can spare you from suffering, even for a short time, it's worth any sacrifice I have to make."

My voice shook as I struggled not to lose myself. "It's terrible all the dragon shifters are gone. I can't bear it. I'm the last dragon shifter in the world. I'm all that's left. I..."

I took a quivering breath, then forced out, "But we can't change it. If this is the fate of the dragon shifters, at least now I can be with you."

"Why would you want to be? I lied to you." Gianna sniffed.

"I'm not angry at you for hiding the truth. Everything's happened so fast, and I understand that you didn't want to hurt me."

I grabbed her hands. "But this is our *chance*. If I can't achieve my dream, at least we can be together, like we should be."

She shoved my hands away. "No, Deryn. You still can't stay, because if all the dragon shifters are dead, that means Helis will be hunting *you*, too. He won't stop until all the dragon shifters are extinct, because he's afraid of them. That means he's afraid of you. You won't be safe until you leave the kingdom for good... which means you'll have to leave me behind. I've vowed to serve the Oracle all my days. I won't go back on that promise now." She dropped her head.

I lifted her chin gently, so her eyes locked with mine. "I'd rather die at home with you, fighting at your side, young and more in love than I ever have been, than live a thousand lives without knowing your name."

Gianna hitched a breath. She closed her eyes and I leaned in, desperately wanting to put my mouth upon hers, needing to forget that my dream was lost and all the horrible things that had happened. Our faces came closer, our lips nearly brushing together. Gianna gave a soft sigh, leaning in further.

Let me kiss you, Gianna. Let me love you the way you

deserve to be loved. For a single, precious moment, I thought we would.

"Well, I didn't think I'd find the two of you here like this."

I knew that voice. Gianna and I sprang apart as ice rushed through my veins. I jumped to my feet, readying myself to fight... to kill.

Standing there with a cocky spark in his eye, a smug smile on his face was my brother— *Helis.*

CHAPTER SEVEN
GIANNA

My hand immediately went to the sword on my hip. Deryn squared his shoulders, poised to shift into the terrifying beast he was.

Helis threw his hands up, indicating he was unarmed. "Whatever Alion told you is a lie!"

I stayed alert for the loyalists I'd seen him with in the temple, but it appeared that he was alone. That made no sense. Why would he come here without his men?

Deryn's shoulders shook in rage, as if he was struggling to hold his magic back. "So help me, I will char your bones to ashes before you take another breath."

"I didn't try to kill Alion!" Helis rushed to explain. "This is all a mistake! I'm here because I'm trying to save my own life!"

"Prove it," Deryn snarled. "I'm not believing anything you say unless you give me proof."

"Just hear me out," Helis pleaded. "After Father died, I found records that showed I was the true first-born."

"And why should we believe you?" I asked.

"Because it's the *truth!*" he cried. "I presented the evidence to Alion before the coronation. He had no idea I was the heir to the throne, and he thought I had fabricated records to try to steal the crown."

"That's why you stabbed him," Deryn accused. "Then you fled, and you decided to take me down with you. Alion was planning to *execute* me!"

"No!" Helis insisted. "I didn't stab Alion. He staged the assassination attempt himself in order to get me arrested. I fled because he set me up."

"That's ridiculous," Deryn sneered. "Alion would never stab *himself*."

"To frame me, he would," Helis countered. "You have to believe me."

"What about your notes about the line of succession? You circled the part in the law book about the throne passing down to the next sibling in line if the first was unfit to rule, then wrote *this is the way*," Deryn hissed.

"When I read that book, I realized *Father* must've proposed that I was unfit to rule to the rest of his council, so he could install Alion as king instead of me, despite me being firstborn," Helis argued. "It was *his* plan I was unveiling, not mine!"

I stepped toward him, aiming my sword straight at his throat. "I saw you in the temple last night. You kidnapped Rana."

Helis furrowed his brow. "What use would I have of a sphinx?"

"She's the Oracle," I spat. "You have every use of her."

Helis shook his head. "I couldn't have been in the temple last night, because it took me all day and through the night to make the journey here on foot."

"I *saw* you in your sun-embroidered cloak," I accused. "You and your brother have different eyes, just like you have different birthmarks."

"A simple potion can change a person's eye color. Alion could've taken one to disguise himself." Helis gestured down to his plain cotton clothing. He hadn't even fled with armor. "If it were me in that temple, then where is my cloak now? It must've been Alion posing as me. He already made everyone believe I tried to kill him. Why not frame me for kidnapping the Oracle as well?"

"The absence of your cloak proves nothing," Deryn sneered.

"Then perhaps this will." Helis reached into a leather bag on his hip to withdraw a scroll. He gently tossed the scroll in our direction, and it rolled across the ground at my feet.

Deryn remained ready to attack if his brother made any moves. I carefully sheathed my sword and bent to inspect the scroll. As I unrolled it, the authenticity of the record became apparent. The paper was delicate and looked at least twenty years old. The official seal of the palace had been placed at the top.

I scanned the records and found that Helis was telling the truth— at least, the part about being the eldest born son. A vision filled my head as I grasped the scroll, and I tumbled into the past.

I saw King Severin meeting with his council, each of them sitting around a long square table, wine goblets laid out for each to drink.

"Helis is weak, and has too many ideas. That child will lead the country into chaos. Yet Alion shows great promise. He follows my orders without question and is in line with my vision for the future. Therefore, he is the one who will follow my path," Severin told his advisors. "Helis might be firstborn, and Alion may be second in line for the crown, but to get what I desire, Alion must be first."

"If Helis is unnecessary, the child does not have to survive," one of the advisors suggested.

King Severin frowned. "Helis is necessary should anything happen to Alion. My bloodline must survive, and I'd sooner kill anyone who knows the truth about the twins' birth order than kill my own son. I will conceal the records of the twins' birth and ensure that Alion is presented to the kingdom as the first-born."

"And what about the queen?" another questioned. "She will oppose this arrangement. What is to be done with her?"

"My wife has never been very compliant. Fortunately, she is due to take a visit to her sister within the Alype Mountains within the week. Those paths are treacherous, full of snow and thieves. Bandits could run upon her carriage and court at any time. I've warned her not to go time and again, but she is determined to make the trip."

Severin picked up his goblet. "She has given me three sons. That is enough to secure the monarchy, and rid myself of this irritating marriage. I've already dealt with the nursemaids and midwives who were there at the time of the twins' birth. They have found themselves out of the employment of... life, really. But you all know this must stay between us."

"Yes, my Lord," the same advisor responded. "We will not tell a soul."

The king gave a twisted smile. "Of course you won't. Cheers to the kingdom, and to the true ruler of our nation!"

King Severin lifted a goblet of wine, and the others followed his lead. As soon as they brought the wine to their lips, they began sputtering in unison. The advisors choked as blood oozed from their mouths, and within moments, they had all slumped to the table, dead.

The vision ended, and I brought myself back to the present. "Helis is right. He *was* the firstborn. Your father made the switch and killed everyone who knew the truth."

"Why would Father do that?" Deryn demanded.

"Alion was more compliant and did whatever Father said, even when we were children," Helis stated. "Father must've made the switch before we were old enough to remember, and we believed the lie."

"That's not all." My voice cracked as I added, "I'm sorry, but Severin killed your mother. The bandit ambush in the Alype Mountains wasn't a random attack. Severin sent the bandits after the queen, so she'd be unable to confront Severin once he put Alion in the line of succession instead of Helis."

Deryn's eyes sparked with tears as he whispered, "That asinine madman."

I ached at his pain, and his fists clenched tightly as he held off waves of grief. Helis merely stared at the ground, void of feeling, as if he'd already suspected this and just needed to know for sure.

I rolled up the scroll and held my hand out to Helis. "I need to confirm the rest of your story."

Deryn yanked me back. "He won't touch you!"

"He must," I argued. "These records are authentic, but I need to use my magic to see if he's telling the truth about the rest of it."

"I am unarmed, brother." Helis spun around slowly to prove he had no blades. "If she must touch me to gain your trust, then she may."

Deryn hesitated, but he finally dropped his hand from my arm. "If you harm her in any way, I *will* end you."

Helis nodded. "Very well."

I took Helis' hand in mine. In my mind's eye, I saw him fleeing from the palace. He didn't even have time to grab a horse from the stables. The sun beat down on him as he stumbled across the countryside, then darkness fell before he made it to the Shadowed Range. He'd been right that he didn't have time to return to the temple last night.

I thought of what I'd witnessed in that temple. The rage I'd seen on Helis' face then was nothing like the devastation I saw in his eyes now. It was almost like I was looking at a different person, and I knew then that I *was*.

I'd told Deryn that Helis had yelled at a guard when he bumped into him. Alion had been injured by a dagger wound to the shoulder that he'd inflicted upon himself, to frame Helis. Only an injury like that would explain why he had snapped at his guard so quickly. Alion had been the one wearing the sun-embroidered cloak, posing as Helis, and he'd reacted in pain when the guard touched his injured shoulder.

"He's telling the truth," I said.

Deryn narrowed his eyes. "Explain yourself. All of it. How did you come across these records?"

"Father had been searching for the home of the dragon shifters for many years," Helis explained. "This place is called Embervale. Father consulted with Alion and I about his plans to track the dragon shifters down, but he forbade us to talk with you about it. I thought that he wanted it to be a surprise, but as time went on, I realized he was hiding it from you on purpose. Several days before his death, he told us the dragon shifters had been discovered, but I had a bad feeling about what he was going to do. So I stayed behind and hid, eavesdropping on him as he spoke to Alion in secret within the meeting chambers. I'll never forget what he said. *Deryn's ambitions are getting out of hand. No son of mine will abandon me for some pathetic dream.*"

Deryn's expression had been enraged, but now, it was so vacant... so cold. All the fire had been extinguished in him at his father's words, and it tore me apart to witness.

Helis shrugged. "I didn't understand what he meant at the time. Then Father died, and I had a chance to tell you the truth. I wanted to tell you about Embervale, because Father could no longer stop me. He hadn't told me where to find it, so I went to the royal records to figure out where it could be. It was there that I stumbled upon the truth of my birth."

"We found your secret hideout," Deryn added. "You had a map marked with this location. You inscribed the words, *Here is the best spot.* You knew all along."

"I swear to the gods I didn't," Helis countered. "That map was among the items I found in the royal records. There were many maps marked, but I kept the one you found because I believed it was the location of the dragon city. I was unable to go back for the map after I fled Alion's chambers, but I remembered where it led. It's how I found my way here."

"Honest men don't keep records in secret hideouts," Deryn accused.

"I had to hide everything from Father. You know Alion was always Father's favorite, because he did as he was told without question. I was never like that, even as a child. I wanted to become a historian, but Father insisted I had to be a prince. I used to sneak into the royal library to study, but I was caught one too many times. Father ordered six lashings— one for every book I had taken."

Helis tore off his shirt and displayed his back to us. My insides churned as I witnessed six long stripes across his skin, proof of the horror his father had inflicted upon him. Deryn cringed, but didn't look away.

"I didn't let you, or anyone else, see them. I only swam within the waters of the Pool of Kenory, and bathed in private to conceal the markings, because I was ashamed," Helis explained. "I was young then, and I learned early on that I couldn't let Father see me pursue my passion. I even had to sneak off to the Pool of Kenory because Father didn't approve of my interests. He said history was a job for lowly scribes, not a prince like me. He wanted me to be interested in war, battle and conquest, like Alion was, but I didn't care for those things. I kept journals and first-hand accounts of everything I saw at the Pool because I wanted nothing more than to be a historian, but I had to hide my records in a secret passageway away from Father. If he knew I was continuing my research in private, the torture would've continued."

"After everything Father lied about, why would you come to Embervale?" Deryn asked.

"I thought the dragon shifters could help me," Helis said. "I assumed I might be able to forge some sort of alliance to prove my innocence, or at the very least, seek refuge outside the kingdom. But when I got here... all the dragons were already gone. Father didn't want you to leave Mystic Peak, so he sent soldiers here to destroy your dream himself."

Deryn's lips trembled. "That can't be true. Father

promised me years ago that he would use his resources to find the dragon city, so I could be united with my kind."

Helis dropped his gaze. "Father promised you he'd *find* the dragon city. He never said what he'd do once he found it."

Deryn stumbled back a step. I could see the betrayal written on his face, but beneath it, he couldn't deny his brother's claim. King Severin had deceived his son and destroyed an entire people. If the king wasn't already dead, I would've taken his life myself for what he'd done.

"I didn't know Father planned to destroy the dragon shifters," Helis added. "It wasn't until I got here that I realized what he'd done."

"How did you get through the mountain range?" I asked. "The terrain is too treacherous for a journey on foot."

"When Father found the city, he revealed to me that he'd found safe passage through a cave system, one that the dragon shifters spent decades reinforcing and concealing for their own transportation," Helis said. "I found hundreds of footprints when I came in. It's how our father's men snuck in and slaughtered the people of Embervale."

Helis reached into his bag again. "There's one more thing. I found this in the wreckage of the village."

He pulled out a leather-bound book that looked a lot

like grimoires I'd seen in the temple. The edges were burnt, but most of the pages remained intact.

Helis opened it to a page covered in soot, though the ink writings were still legible. "I found it in the dragon's temple. It was open to a page on curses. This one describes the exact way Father died. Gasping for air, welts on his skin, withering away for days before finally perishing in a horrible death."

Deryn swallowed audibly. "The dragons must've used their magic to curse Father while he was attacking their city, but it took time to take effect. Do you think any of them made it out alive?"

"If they did, they're long gone now," Helis stated. "If there's any chance of finding survivors, you'd need an Oracle to lead you to them."

"And now Alion's got her." I sneered his name in disgust. "You two know your brother best. Is there anywhere in the realm Alion could be holding Rana?"

"There are dungeons back in the palace," Deryn said. "But he wants Helis to take the fall for Rana's disappearance, so he'd probably conceal her somewhere that has no direct ties to himself. He'd want to lock her in a magical prison. She's too powerful to keep inside the castle."

"I found historical records alongside this spellbook," Helis noted. "They mentioned someplace high in the mountains within a cave system. The dragons avoid it because it contains powerful crystals that can trap a magical creature. If I were Alion, that's where I'd take her, but I'd never heard of these caves before, and I'm not sure Alion knew of them, either. There are so many cave systems throughout the kingdom, but I've never seen crystals like these records describe."

Deryn got a thoughtful look on his face. "What kind of crystals?"

"The records indicate they're *crystals like fire.*"

Realization crossed Deryn's features. "You haven't seen them because you never went far enough into the caves to witness them, but I have... and so did Alion. It's the same place he used to leave me when we played there as kids— a place even I as a dragon shifter couldn't escape. Alion has taken the sphinx to the Cryptic Caves."

CHAPTER EIGHT
DERYN

"Are you sure about this?" Gianna called over the wind as we flew toward the Cryptic Caves. She sat on my back, and so did Helis, as I carried them over the mountains and to where I was certain the sphinx was being kept.

"I don't know anywhere else that's powerful enough to keep the Oracle contained. Alion must be using those crystals to imprison her. Her power would've helped her escape otherwise."

I saw the gaping mouth of the cave's entrance below. I dropped down, landing outside the cave. Gianna and Helis slid off my back, and I changed into a man. We entered the cave, keeping a sharp eye out for Alion or any of his men.

The caverns inside the cave were wide and tall enough that I could walk through them in my dragon form if I wished. Torches that were mounted on the walls provided light, blazing with fire.

I looked closer at the torches and saw that they were freshly lit. "Someone's been here recently. I'll bet anything Alion's still around."

"Then let's make him pay for taking the Oracle." Gianna's grip tightened on her sword, and we forged onward.

As we got further into the cave, the walls began to glow ruby red. Large crystals, taller than a man, sprouted from the rock at all angles, providing glimmering light. As I approached the crystals, I felt my dragon magic begin to wane.

"These crystals absorb magical energy." I laid my hand upon one of the crystals, then recoiled, wincing as I felt it drain my fire. "The Oracle wouldn't be able to foresee visions or use her magic while surrounded by these stones."

"I can't get any visions, either. My psychic abilities are completely locked down," Gianna said.

"Then we're going to have to free her the old-fashioned way." Helis strung a bow with a sharp arrow. We'd stopped along the way to obtain weapons in a town that was between Embervale and Mystic Peak. If we couldn't use magic, it was a fool's errand to go against Alion unarmed. I gripped a steel sword that I'd forged with my fire years ago and hid in the woods, just in case I ever needed it. I was glad I'd had the foresight to come up with a contingency plan if I needed to defend myself, though I never would've thought Alion would be the one staging the coup.

The caverns came to an end, widening into a massive epichamber. In the center of this gigantic cavern was a broad cage, and within it was the sphinx.

Rana was a gorgeous creature. She had the body of a lion and the golden wings of an eagle, the head of the most beautiful woman in the realm atop her shoulders. Her long black hair went flowing down her back, her features perfectly painted by the gods despite wearing no makeup.

Usually, being in Rana's presence was enough to bring most people to their knees, because she was that powerful. Even non-magical people could feel the magic echoing off her form at all times. But that power seemed subdued now by the power of the surrounding crystals.

"Rana!" Gianna cried out, tears in her eyes. She ran toward the cage, kneeling beside the door as she gazed upward at her mentor in reverence. "You're alive!"

"*I am well, my child,*" the Oracle replied in her mystical voice, her words resonating with strength. "*Though I could not break free of this cage to find you. These crystals prevent me from harnessing my abilities.*"

"We'll get you out of there," Gianna promised, and she began yanking on the bars. I attempted to use my dragon strength to yank off the lock as I had previously, but it wouldn't budge. Down here, I was as strong as any common man, and that wasn't enough to break Rana out of her cage.

"I knew you'd eventually come for her. You walked right into my trap."

A deep voice made a shudder roll throughout my bones, and the three of us turned. Alion was standing there, cloaked in a dark red robe with my father's crown already on his head.

He didn't deserve it. He needed to give it *back*.

I noticed one of his shoulders was slumped— the one that was injured when he'd stabbed himself. In his hand, he held a golden key.

"Looking for this?" Alion showed the key to us, then pocketed it in his robe. "It's the only way to let the sphinx out. Too bad you'll never get it off of me."

"It's over, Alion." Helis faced his twin, raising the bow to point an arrow at our brother. "You are not the rightful heir to the throne. Now stand down."

Alion emitted a cruel laugh. "This is far from over."

Helis unleashed the arrow, but Alion dodged out of the way. The bolt hit the stone wall behind him and shattered.

"You're a poor fighter, Helis. You would've been an even poorer king. No wonder I was Father's favorite."

Alion smirked. It made me want to punch the smug look off his face.

"You didn't need to bring Rana into this," I growled. "You should've kept the Oracle out of your games of power."

"I took the sphinx because I needed to obtain a vision on where Helis went," Alion hissed. "I needed to track him down before the information about our birth got out, and she was the only way to do so."

"So you could imprison me? Kill me?" Helis demanded.

"Father insisted *I* was the rightful ruler! Something as silly as birth order should never be considered when determining the fate of a kingdom. You were obsessed with your books and your scrolls, while I was concerned with making our nation magnificent."

"Making it larger, you mean," Helis accused. "You wanted to continue Father's work, and wage war against kingdoms that didn't belong to you so you could conquer them and expand Mystic Peak's territory, instead of forging allies to create peace."

Alion shrugged. "Why make peace when I can bring everything in the continent under my domain? It makes no sense. Father was a grand conqueror, but I will be even greater."

"*Your plans for utter control of the realm will not end in triumph, Alion. I witnessed the moon rising over the sun, and so, believed King Severin's lie that you were born first. But now I see my vision was misinterpreted. You have come before your brother to take the throne not because it belongs to you, but because you have sought to claim it unjustly for yourself. It will not work. Helis will rule, and that is what shall be,"* Rana replied coolly.

"Silence! You were useless to me. You didn't provide the vision I needed in time," Alion spat.

"Visions do not appear on command when we want them. They are gifts from the gods, and you have stifled my abilities by trapping me within the Cryptic Caves," Rana growled. *"But no matter what you may do, Alion, son of Severin, you will not use me as a tool against the people of this kingdom. I protect Mystic Peak from monsters like you."*

"Your protests are futile, Oracle. I will do away with you, as my father did away with the dragon shifters." Alion swept his robe behind him, preparing to fight.

"Did you help him?" I demanded, taking a step forward as my arms quivered in rage. "Did you storm Embervale and exterminate all those dragons on his orders?"

Alion shook his head. "I didn't know Father had sent soldiers to Embervale until after it happened. He told me the town had been wiped out before he died, but he swore me to keep it a secret from you two. He knew you wouldn't take the news well, and that Helis would go poking his nose around where it didn't belong."

Alion's eyes burned as he glared at his twin. "But you did anyway. And now you're trying to *take* what's rightfully mine, what I've been raised my entire life to become. I didn't need to know that I wasn't the firstborn. Yet you shoved it in my face like some kind of *accomplishment,* when I've been working for decades to become the king you never could be!"

"I wasn't showing that information to you so I could take your crown. I came to you with that knowledge because I'm your twin, and there should be no secrets between us. I wanted you to know that Father lied to us," Helis raged. "You might've been able to convince me to back down and allow you to have the throne anyway, persuaded me to keep this secret, but any possibility of that happening failed when you stabbed yourself and yelled to your guards that I'd attacked you. You framed me, and tried to kill me, then you tried to kill Deryn! Anyone who's capable of slaughtering the people that love him to keep power has no right to rule a kingdom. Someone like that won't put his people first, but himself."

"It doesn't matter what you think, because this ends now," Alion seethed. "The truth about our birth can never get out, and the three of you are the only people left that know. I'll kill all of you before I allow you to take the kingdom from me."

Alion used his good arm to unleash a pair of throwing knives from within his robes, hurling them at his twin. One missed, but the other made an impact. The knife sank into Helis' torso, and he hitched a sharp breath. Helis sank to the ground, gasping as his hands clutched the knife in his side as blood spurted from the wound.

He couldn't fight with an injury like that. He couldn't even walk. He could barely breathe.

As I rushed to help my brother, Alion redirected his attention toward the sphinx. Alion withdrew more knives from his robes, tossing them at the Oracle. She dodged the blades as some of them hit the bars, but others sailed through the gaps and sliced through her coat. Blood sprayed the bars, and Rana cried out in pain.

"You won't harm her!" Gianna reacted, springing to stop Alion and drawing her sword arm back. She swung for his neck, but he ducked and smacked her across the face. The sword went skittering out of her hand, and he yanked Gianna to him. She laid dazed against his chest.

"Gianna!" All thought and reason fled from my mind as I realized she was in danger. I sprinted toward her, but came to an abrupt halt as Alion lifted a knife and placed it against her throat.

Gianna visibly swallowed, her skin going pale. Alion

grinned. "I might consider letting the pretty girl go. But you two will always be a threat to me unless you're gone. It doesn't matter if the truth about our birth gets out if all the other heirs are dead."

"What are you saying?" My entire body trembled. I wanted to shift so *badly,* but with the power of these crystals holding me back, I couldn't. He was too far away for me to reach Gianna in time if he decided to end her now.

Alion raised an eyebrow. "Your little courtship wasn't as big a secret as you believed it to be. I know you love her. The only question is, how much?"

"Don't you dare." The fire within me was raging, begging to be let out so I could destroy him where he stood. No one laid hands on Gianna as long as I breathed... yet she was at Alion's mercy, and one false move could take her from me.

The fire from the torchlight danced off Alion's face, casting it in shadow. "Here's my proposition. Deryn, you can kill Helis, and then yourself. In exchange, I'll let Gianna live. Or you can try to fight me, and I'll slit her throat before you even get close. Which will you choose?"

CHAPTER NINE
GIANNA

I could feel my pulse pounding against the blade of the knife. All Alion had to do was press downward slightly, and he'd finish me off. I'd never seen Deryn look so terrified. He was about to fall to his knees, to beg his brother not to kill me.

Alion was a coward. He knew he couldn't win in a fight against Deryn, so he was using me as a bargaining chip.

But Deryn wouldn't. He'd never sacrifice an entire kingdom for me.

Except... that's not what Deryn's eyes said. He backed away, glancing at Helis as if considering doing what Alion asked.

Shock rooted me to the spot, and I went limp against Alion's hold. I didn't realize how much Deryn loved me.

I knew he cared. But I didn't know I was his entire *world*.

Deryn's life was at stake, and so was mine. I had to think of a way out of this, and fast.

"Wait. You don't want to kill me. The Oracle doesn't have enough power to foresee visions in these caves, but *I* do," I lied. "I can give you whatever you want."

"Prove it," Alion snarled. "Why should I trust what you say?"

"I saw you kidnap the sphinx that night, and I let you do it," I said. "A guard bumped into your hurt arm at the temple, and you cried out in pain. I watched you put her into iron chains and drag her away. And I did nothing to save her. I let you take her hostage."

"If that's true, why didn't you try and stop me?"

"Because I knew if I brought Helis and Deryn to you, that you would reward me. You're already king. And as king, you can give me anything I desire if I serve you." I kept my voice even, playing the part of the traitor. "You know my past, that I was orphaned as a child. I had nothing until the Oracle took me in. I refuse to go back to that life. Nothing is worth falling into poverty again, and if I have to be cruel to others to avoid that fate, so be it. But I can't save myself if I don't elevate my station, and being a sorceress for the Oracle isn't enough. If I'm cast out of the temple for any reason, I'll lose everything. I need to make sure that never happens."

I heard Alion swallow. "Yes. That's completely understandable. I would do the same."

He couldn't imagine a worse fate than having no money or status, even if he had to give up his family to maintain what he had. What a sick man.

"I knew you would be king, the strongest ruler who had ever lived. Some time ago, I foresaw you years in the future, and knew what you would become."

"What did you foresee?" His words were greedy with thoughts of what the future could be.

I just had to tell him what he wanted to hear. "You had conquered the entire realm, and no other kingdom existed besides the one that you ruled over. The people called you the greatest king of Mystic Peak there ever was or would be."

A slight hint of darkness fell from his voice. "And why should I believe any of this? You could just be trying to save Deryn's skin."

"I only pretended to love Deryn so I could get closer to attaining my ambitions. Marrying a prince would give me power beyond belief. But you're king now, so it doesn't matter if Deryn knows I don't love him. He loves me, and he'll still die to protect me. But power is more valuable than any love this world offers. Give me a place in your court as a noble lady, riches and status beyond belief, and I'll use my visions to serve this new kingdom you plan to create."

Alion mused on this. "Perhaps you could be of use to me after all. Though I won't let you live unless Deryn exchanges his life for yours, and takes Helis out with him."

"Helis is already dying from your blade, and Deryn will do whatever I ask," I promised. "It would be a waste to kill a dragon whom you could use to conquer the realm. Whole armies could fall by his fire alone, and Deryn will follow your orders so long as I'm the one who gives them. You don't need the Oracle anymore, because you have me. Kill her, then imprison Deryn in the cell until he agrees to follow your orders. It won't take long. He's too infatuated with me to deny my requests for long."

"It seems like a good plan. But you went to defend the sphinx when I attacked her. Why would you do such a thing if you wish to take her place?"

"Because I can take her power. She's my mentor. Whatever power she possesses will pass on to me, but I have to absorb her magic first before she dies. Otherwise, it'll be lost." Alion had no knowledge of how psychic abilities worked. Only the temple sorceresses were permitted to be taught our secrets. I had to use that to my advantage.

Alion made a small noise of agreement. "I didn't think you were so cunning, but you've proven yourself to be wise. Very well. I'll open the cell so you can absorb the Oracle's power, then we'll kill the sphinx. You can shove Deryn into the cage afterward, and *that one* can bleed out for all I care." Alion gestured toward Helis.

Slowly, he removed the blade from my neck. I didn't go to harm him or pick up my sword, which convinced him I was telling the truth.

He dug in his pocket, then handed the key to me. "Open the cell."

I took the key. With Alion's knife at my back, I proceeded toward the cage that the sphinx was trapped in. I inserted the key into the lock, my eyes connecting with Rana's.

We only had seconds. Alion pointed the knife into my back, and I felt a speck of blood begin to stain my cloak. "What's taking so long? Claim her power!"

I held my breath, then grabbed the door and swung it open. Rana reared back on her hind legs and pounced. She didn't have her magic, but she still had her claws. When she opened her human-like mouth, daggerish teeth like those of a great cat gleamed in her jaws. She sailed over me, landing on Alion and digging her claws in.

Alion cried out in pain. He swung the knife, but Rana batted it out of his hand. She reached down and sank her teeth into Alion's neck, dragging him off to a crevice in the cave floor. Alion's petrified screams could be heard as Rana pulled him into the depths of the cave, his desperate pleas echoing across the walls until abruptly, they stopped.

There was the padding of paws upon stone, then Rana emerged from the crevice, blood dripping from her mouth. *"When he was born, I foresaw that the Cryptic Caves would be Alion's final resting place. I did not know it was I who would leave him here, but he was a threat to the kingdom, and therefore, shall be no more."*

"Gianna." Deryn rushed to me, sweeping me into his arms. He brushed back my hair. I held him tightly, trembling against his embrace. We'd nearly lost each other, but somehow, we'd managed to stop Alion. He could never hurt us again.

Except the true heir to the throne was already dying. Helis writhed against the floor, foam spitting out of his mouth as he bled. We scampered to him, and Deryn cradled his brother in his arms.

"He's dying. We need to get him help, or he's not going to make it." Deryn's panicked tone frightened me. If something wasn't done, he'd lose two brothers today.

"Put him upon my back. It is a great honor to help the future king of Mystic Peak," Rana said.

Deryn laid Helis over the back of the sphinx. Rana darted forward as the heir hung limply across her shoulders. *"Come quickly, and follow me."*

Rana raced off into a different part of the cave system, one opposite from the cavern we'd come from.

We didn't ask questions, but Deryn grabbed a nearby torch off the wall to provide light as we entered a deeper part of the cave.

Our footsteps echoed as we entered into another wide space. Multiple voices could be heard all around.

Deryn lifted the torch. I saw that within cells similar to the Oracle's cage were dozens of people, men, women and children. They smelled slightly of ash, had soot on their faces, and the temperature in the cool cavern was warmer than what it should've been from their presence.

"Who are you?" Deryn asked in a bewildered voice, but from the amazement in his tone, he already knew.

"We're dragon shifters, the only survivors of the siege on Embervale. King Severin took us prisoner and kept us here. He planned to turn us into war machines once he brainwashed us into working for him, but he died before he could convert us to his side," one of the dragons said, a young man with long, silver hair. "We can tell that you're one of us. I am Silvon."

"Prince Deryn," he explained. "I'm guessing you can't get yourselves out."

"No. These bars are enchanted, and we can't shift until you let us out of here and lead us away from these crystals. Please, let us out," Silvon pleaded.

I still had the key from Rana's cage. I fit it into the lock on the cell, hoping it would fit. The door swung open easily, and the dragon shifters sighed in relief as they escaped the cell and gathered around us.

Silvon gave a bow. "Thank you, Prince Deryn. If we can help you in any way or offer a reward for freeing us, we will gladly pay it."

"My brother. Please, is there anything you can do?" Deryn asked. He grasped Helis, who was quickly turning gray.

"We can help him," Silvon replied. "Quickly, the exit."

Rana roared, motioning us to follow her. Deryn and I grasped hands and went after her, while the dragon shifters trailed behind us. We escaped the caves, coming out of the mountains onto a flat area surrounded by the peaks and getting far away from the crystals. I felt my psychic abilities surge back once we were out of the Cryptic Caves. Deryn took Helis down from Rana's back, laying him on the ground.

Helis was so pale I figured he was dead already, and that this was beyond hope. But the dragon shifters gathered around Helis in a circle. One by one they began to transform, changing into their dragon shapes. Silvon became a silver dragon, and the rest of the shifters each changed into a spectacular dragon of their own, varying in color and size.

The dragons began to sing, melding their voices into a beautiful harmony as they swayed back and forth, lifting their heads to the skies. As if by instinct, Deryn shifted too, adding his voice to the prayers going up around the mountainside.

That beautiful song carried over the peaks until the sky ignited with fire. I heard the roar of a great beast, and the clouds parted as a bright light emitted from the heavens, shining down upon Helis as red scales flashed amongst the skies.

The dragons' prayers to their god was answered as the god Solfyre bestowed his blessing upon Helis. I watched, amazed, as Helis' wound knit together and repaired itself, becoming whole. Color came back into Helis' cheeks and he sat up slowly, touching the mended cut with awe.

Tears fell from my eyes as the dragons finished their captivating song, and Rana gave a rumble of pride beside me.

"The heir has been restored," Rana growled. *"All hail the true king."*

CHAPTER TEN
DERYN

A fortnight after Alion was slain, Helis' coronation took place. News of what had happened spread quickly across the kingdom. Between the records Helis had presented— which had been authenticated by the royal scribes— and testimony from the Oracle, we were able to prove beyond a shadow of a doubt that Helis was the true heir to the throne. I too was exonerated from all alleged crimes.

Through the investigation, it was revealed that General Skyglade was the one to lead the king's army to Embervale and command the slaughter of all those people. Helis found records of an ancient treaty signed by Mystic Peak and the surrounding kingdoms that agreed to refrain from combat with vulnerable populations. Since Embervale had been attacked unprovoked, it was determined that Mystic Peak's army, under King

Severin's rule, violated the treaty. This was enough to strip General Skyglade of his rank, and he fled the kingdom shortly afterward. Rana was certain no one would hear from him ever again.

The coronation was a grand celebration, opening with the sound of trumpets whose melody echoed all throughout the town. The crowd surrounding the temple grounds where the ceremony was taking place was so large that it spanned throughout the town.

As the highest-ranking spiritual leader in the kingdom, Rana had the honor of placing the crown upon Helis' head. It was different from the silver crown with red velvet that my father had worn during his reign, the one Alion had died wearing. A new crown had been forged from gold and embedded with precious yellow gems that glowed like the sun. This one was specially made for Helis, to signify the beginning of a new era.

Gianna and I were seated at the front of the temple, surrounded by the dragon shifters we'd rescued from the Cryptic Caves. Helis had personally invited them to the coronation himself as his guests of honor.

"This crown is your birthright." Rana projected her voice over the chapel for all in attendance to hear. *"It is the wisdom I imparted at your birth: The moon comes before the sun. Your father used that wisdom to deceive the kingdom into believing you were second born, but in truth, the wisdom indicated that Alion would rule before*

you. His reign was short-lived, but yours will shine bright for many decades to come. For as long as the sun shines in the sky, no darkness can cast out its light."

The temple erupted into cheers as Helis was pronounced king. The crowd outside joined in the celebration until the entire town came alive with joy. The royal clergy began to lead Helis down the aisle for the procession, but he held up a hand to stop them.

"This moment shall not wait," Helis announced. "As my first act as king, I order the area known as Divine Valley to henceforth be declared a safe haven for all dragons."

I went speechless as I watched a large map unfurl from above his head at the front of the temple, depicting a lush and green land. It was far away from the Shadowed Range, on the opposite side of the kingdom but still within Mystic Peak's borders.

I'd never ventured to that area, but I'd heard the name before. It was an area my father had seized many years ago, though he'd never disclosed its exact location. This must've been another map Helis had found in the royal records.

Divine Valley was said to be one of the most beautiful places in all the realm, with endless waterfalls and lush greenery. Father had intended to expand the kingdom and begin a settlement there, but with all the rivers and waterfalls in the area, it was difficult to navigate on foot. The dragons would have no issues traversing the area from the skies, though. It was an immense gift for Helis to bestow upon them— upon *us*.

"Furthermore," Helis added. "By royal decree, all dragons will be granted citizenship within our kingdom effective immediately. The dragons will no longer be forced into hiding, but will be among those we honor and defend."

Silvon fell to his knees before the king. "Your Highness. How may we thank you for this honor?"

"You may go forth and rebuild your population," Helis stated. "From this day and henceforth, we will be known not just as allies, but as citizens of the same nation."

Silvon bowed his head. "Then as you promise to honor and defend us, we swear to do the same for you."

"I have but one final request," Helis said. "Take my brother with you."

All eyes turned to me before I had a moment to process his words. It hadn't occurred to me that I was among the dragon shifters he spoke of.

Silvon gave a reverent nod to the king. "Of course we will, your Majesty. The dragons of Divine Valley will need someone to lead us in building our new city."

"You... want me?" I stammered.

Silvon turned to me. "Our commanders perished

when the city was seized. We could not ask for a better leader than the dragon shifter who freed us."

All around me, dragon shifters dropped to one knee in solidarity. They didn't just want me to join them as a citizen, but to lead them as their duke, one title shy of king.

Helis stepped toward me, reaching out a hand. "Then it is decided. Your journey is just beginning, brother, and you will become a great leader as the Oracle foretold: *An inferno can spark from the smallest ember.* The spark has already been lit, and your inferno awaits. Enjoy the journey, Prince Deryn, Duke of Divine Valley."

My head spun, and the new title barely registered as I tried to take it all in.

Gianna nudged me. "Go ahead, Deryn. It's all you ever wanted."

I couldn't tear myself away from those mesmerizing eyes. There was only one thing I wanted more than to live among the dragons. "Will you come with me?"

Her eyes began to water, but she lifted her hand to place it on my cheek. "You know the answer to that, Deryn. I have always loved you, and I *will* always love you, but my heart says there's more for both of us beyond this calling. If we have to go our separate ways to reach our greatest potential, then we must. You have to take this opportunity— just as we did not know where the

Pool of Kenory would lead us, but we ended up in the right place eventually. We might not know the outcome, but you have to follow your heart. I know your heart belongs to the dragons."

My heart belonged to her, too, but there was a fire that had started burning within me, and my love for her was wrapped in a protective layer of *trust*. I didn't know how this would all play out, but I didn't have to. I just had to take the next step, and we both knew what that had to be. I had to stop pretending as if I could change my fate.

I took Helis' hand. "I accept."

My brother led me to the center of the chapel and lifted my hand into the air, presenting me to the masses with my new title.

I lifted my head high. I didn't want to say goodbye to Gianna, but putting my trust in her had never failed before. It wouldn't fail me now.

Cheers filled the streets, and the trumpets began to play as the procession started. Helis climbed into a grand carriage outside the temple doors, and Gianna and I were ushered into the one behind him. As the prince and one of the highest regarded spiritual leaders in the realm, we were both honored in the parade that followed. Thousands of people lined the streets, waving banners and throwing flowers at our carriage as we passed. Ahead of us, my brother waved at the townsfolk, his crown shimmering over them like true sunlight.

I felt overwhelmed, at first. My future had shifted in an instant, and I was still trying to grasp the concept. Then Gianna reached over to entwine her fingers into mine. My pulse slowed at her touch.

"You are more courageous than you know. You have a bright future ahead of you."

"A future you've foreseen?" I wondered.

"No. A future I can predict because I know *you*. You will do right by the dragon shifters, and I don't need a vision to know it's where you belong."

I squeezed her hand back. "And you belong with the Oracle. I shouldn't have pressured you into leaving with me. I trust you, Gianna, and if you think this is what's right for both of us, then I will hold on to that belief with all my heart."

The celebrations continued after dark with a feast and dancing at the palace. I didn't think about how Gianna and I would be parting in the morning, because I wanted every last second I had with her to count. I spun her around the dance floor, and she laughed gleefully as I took her in my arms.

The ball was coming to a close when the sphinx approached us. "*I cannot be prouder of you both. You have embraced your callings, though you know not where they will lead you. This means that you are ready.*"

"Ready for what?" Gianna asked.

Rana simply turned. *"Follow me."*

We followed her through the darkened streets of Mystic Peak and returned to the temple. It was empty now, but the moonlight that streamed through the stained-glass windows illuminated the entire chapel.

Rana stopped at the altar, where a silk robe had been laid upon it. It was the kind only Oracles wore during temple ceremonies. *"The time has come, Gianna. Kneel before me."*

Gianna gingerly approached the altar, appearing confused. It was clear even her psychic powers couldn't prepare her for what was to come. "The time for what? Rana, I don't understand."

"It is time for you to graduate from your studies," Rana told her. *"You have followed your intuition and completed a quest most would never venture on. You saved lives and freed innocent prisoners. There is nothing more I can teach you. It is time for you to claim your rightful title as an Oracle."*

Gianna's brow furrowed. "There cannot be two Oracles. I will become an Oracle once you die, as it has always been."

"The title of Oracle is reserved for the highest-ranking Seer of a region," Rana said. *"But there is one region within the kingdom I don't oversee, and the dragons need an Oracle to lead their religious ceremonies."*

It was as if my heart grew wings and took flight. "Is this a dream?"

Gianna looked stunned. "Other kingdoms have their own Oracles. I don't see why there can't be more than one. But, Rana... are you sure I'm ready?"

Rana took the silk robe in her paws, her claws digging into the fabric without snagging it. She lifted herself to her hind legs to present the robe. *"That is for you to decide."*

Gianna wiped tears from her cheeks. "I could never understand why my heart was torn in two different directions. I thought I had to choose between becoming an Oracle or following Deryn to the dragon city. I understand now why my heart longed for both... because it was never a question of *how* I was going to make it happen, only if I'd trust myself enough to receive it. We had the answers inside us all along, whispering to us the truth through our desires. We could always have everything we wanted, but we had to be open to it happening in unexpected ways."

Gianna stepped forward. "I am ready. I accept the title of Oracle, and I will go with Deryn to Divine Valley to preside over the dragon shifters, as Oracle of their region."

Gianna slipped her arms into the silk robe, and something magnificent happened when Rana placed it on her shoulders. The robe began to glow a silvery hue, and wisps of magic swirled upward from Gianna's feet, reaching to the high ceiling like a magical beacon.

It was a sign from the gods. They accepted this declaration and approved Gianna among the ranks of Oracles.

I raced up the steps to the altar the same time Gianna ran for me. I scooped her into my arms and spun her around. The fire within my heart blazed as she squeezed me back tightly. All the magic in the entire realm could've flooded through me in that moment and it wouldn't have felt as enchanting as holding her close, knowing our futures had converged. We could finally be *together*.

Gianna buried her head in my shoulder. "I love you, Deryn. I've loved you for a long time. I want nothing more than to build a future with you."

"My heart desires to share every moment of it in your presence," I whispered.

Then Gianna did something I wasn't even sure the Oracle saw coming. She placed her hands on either side of my face and drew me in for a kiss.

The sparks that flew between us could've devoured the entire town if they hadn't been contained within our chests. Her kiss drove me delirious, and I felt my reality crumbling around me and then knitting itself back together again. For a brief moment, the two of us were all that existed in this world, held together by an unmatched passion and the promise of a beautiful future. I kissed her again, and her mouth roamed over mine like she was trying to memorize the taste of my soul. We were forced to draw away, driven only by the need for breath.

I pushed a strand of red hair behind her ear. "You mean it, then? You'll be our Oracle, help me lead the dragon shifters, and be my mate?"

"Prince Deryn, I will be your *everything*." Gianna kissed me again, and my desperation flared. It seemed that no future would ever be long enough to satisfy my full desire for her.

I knew then that Gianna and I would be a powerful united force. No matter how lost we found ourselves, we would always find our way. Maybe that wasn't a way back home, but rather toward a brighter future. For nothing was ever truly lost.

Only yet to be discovered.

THE END

Read another fantasy novella by Megan Linski in *Dragon Seeker* and a paranormal novella by Alicia Rades in *Murder at the Magic Academy*.

Turn the page to read the first chapters!

DRAGON SEEKER
CHAPTER ONE

I had thought my life couldn't get any worse, until I woke up imprisoned in a tower.

This is what you get for being pessimistic, Leila. My hands and feet were in shackles, chained to a stone wall, and there was straw all over the floor. The only light in the room came from a small window twenty feet above me, which shone a spotlight on a singular purple stone in the middle of the floor.

The worst part about it was that I couldn't remember how I'd gotten here. I'd fallen asleep in my bed the night before, in the girls' dorms at Riveroak University, and now, I was here.

I tried to remember the events of the day before, to provide an explanation as to why I was chained up in some dungeon master's domain. I'd had a full day of classes that I was failing at the university, and had a horrible evening working as a cashier at Happy Burger—which, by the way, was *never* a very happy place to be. I'd been yelled at by grumpy customers the entire day, and when I got home, I had to deal with my bitchy roommate Jenny accusing me of sleeping with her boyfriend behind her back before she stormed out.

I wasn't. My roomate's boyfriend was fugly as fuck, and had a personality to match, not to mention I'd overheard her complaining the other day his dick was smaller than her pinky toe, so I certainly didn't want him. Even so, coming back to my dorm to be yelled at by Jenny for two hours after the shitty day I'd had didn't help. Afterward, I'd numbed my brain by bingewatching my favorite show, stuffing down chocolates before sobbing myself to sleep like a sad sack, wondering how I was going to fix my life and insisting to myself things couldn't sink any lower.

Well, obviously they can, because now some weirdo is holding you captive in his elaborate basement. Was this some BDSM thing I'd forgotten about? I'd never *tried* anything like that before, but I guess I had one too many drinks at the last college party I went to, so who knew what I'd volunteered for at the time.

Was this Jenny's way of getting back at me? If so, this was extreme. Or maybe I'd signed up for some sorority without thinking about it, and this was an initiation. I was pretty desperate for friends, so perhaps I'd signed some sort of interest form for Greek life at the start of the semester, and they were coming to collect now.

I pulled at the shackles, thinking they were fake, but they didn't break. They were definitely real, very heavy, and made of iron. If this was a joke, someone had gone out of their way to pull one on me.

I needed to escape, before whatever psycho brought me here showed up. My attention changed to focus on the stone instead. As it was the only item in the room, I figured I could use it as a way to get myself free, or utilize it as a weapon. The stone was fairly large, at least as big as my backpack, and had a shiny exterior like glass. It appeared to be a giant gemstone. My face reflected back at me, betraying how scared I was.

Okay, Leila, get it together. This isn't as scary as half of the things you've been through. I can think of three things that are way more terrifying than this— like, calculus, or making a phone call to your mother, or melting in your seat at a coffee shop while your putrid ex complains about how much he misses you, when really, he just misses you washing his shit-stained underwear. You'd rather be chained up here than do any of those things.

That was fair, because I *had* done all of those things recently, and I would prefer to be here instead. My expression in the reflection of the stone began to change, and I watched as a crack began to form across the surface.

I held my breath. The crack in the stone grew until pieces of it began falling away. I realized that the stone wasn't a stone at all, but actually an *egg*, and it was hatching!

I was terrified of what might emerge. Some kind of big bird, right? Birds hatched from eggs. But the biggest egg I'd ever seen came from an ostrich, and this egg was much bigger. Was this going to be some sort of terrifying teradactyl?

That might be cool. I was into dinosaurs. I had the momentary thought of how cool it would be if *I* was the person who rediscovered the dinosaurs, and had a *very* stupid image pop into my head of me riding on the back of a giant pterosaur before the egg suddenly exploded.

Fragments of the egg went everywhere. I turned my face away to shield my eyes, then slowly opened them again to face whatever had emerged. When I saw the little creature standing in the remnants of the egg, a huge smile spread across my face.

It wasn't a dinosaur... it was a *dragon*. A reptile the size of a small dog stood across from me, scales a shining amethyst with leathery wings folded across its back. The dragon had a pointed face, straight silver horns, and dazzling, gem-like eyes. Thin membranes from the egg still coated its body. When the dragon saw me, it blinked its large eyes, and waved its arrow-head tail.

The dragon began waddling toward me, taking stumbling steps. I pressed my back against the wall, but fear turned into love as the baby dragon crawled onto my lap, making soft cooing sounds and rubbing its head against my belly.

Did this dragon just... *imprint* on me? Did it think I was its mother? I looked closer. Although I didn't see any indicators of gender, I had the *certainty* that this creature was a girl.

The dragon jumped up to lick my face with a forked tongue, and my heart absolutely melted. Oh my gosh. She was *so cute*. I couldn't bear it!

I didn't understand how this could be true. This was a *real animal*. I could tell by looking at her, by the way she moved, how her scales felt. This wasn't a prank or a dream. But dragons were the stuff of fairy tales. How could they really exist?

She nudged at my hand, but I said, "I'm sorry. These shackles prevent me from petting you."

The little dragon let out a huff. I yelped as she opened her mouth, and flames emitted from it. The flames covered the shackles, but didn't burn me at all. The shackles melted off of me, leaving my wrists and ankles free.

Either this was the discovery of a lifetime, or there'd

been some major drugs in those chocolates I ate last night. I stood with the baby dragon in my arms, cradling her against my chest. "Thank you so much for freeing me. I wish I knew your name."

Ametine. The moniker popped into my head almost instantly, as if the dragon could break into my mind and read my very thoughts.

I patted her spiky head. "Okay, Ametine. How do we get out of here?"

I looked around for an exit, but I didn't even see a door. How the hell had they brought me in here? Around me were nothing but walls.

A shadow fell from the window overhead, and Ametine chirped. I looked up. I gasped as I saw a man standing in the window, looming over me.

The figure jumped, falling the twenty foot span and rolling into a crouch. The man rose, clenching his hands into fists.

Wow. How did he fall like that without breaking his legs? That was *very* impressive.

The stranger strode toward me with his big, broad shoulders thrown back, and I took in his features with awe. He had brown skin, with long hair that was slicked back, falling around his beautiful face. A black beard was precisely trimmed around his sharp jawline and angled cheekbones. He was dressed in leather armor, a cloak falling off his shoulders, while two daggers were holstered to his sides. His clothes clung to every inch of him, showing off his chiseled muscles.

And those eyes... they were so tormented and *deep*. There were a million stories inside those eyes, and I wanted to be told every one.

This man was gorgeous. The handsomest guy at my school would've appeared hideous next to him.

And I was alone with him, locked in a tower with no escape.

"Who are you?" I whispered.

When the words fell from his lips, I found they stole my breath away. "My name is Tiago Altavilla, and I am here to kill you."

Continue the story by reading Dragon Seeker by Megan Linski!

MURDER AT THE MAGIC ACADEMY

CHAPTER ONE

I always knew when something bad was going to happen, and the dark storm clouds brewing above Thornshire only intensified the chill creeping down my spine. I'd lived in a town full of witches all my life, yet Halloween never failed to give me the creeps.

"There's nothing to be afraid of, Elodie." I spoke the words out loud, as if the sound of my own name might help convince me.

Although the eerie feeling told me I should be cautious, I didn't *trust* the instinct. I had to believe the hairs rising on my arms were a result of the brisk weather and not an ominous warning. This wouldn't be the first time my intuition was wrong. Even if this sensation *meant* something, I had no further clues to decipher its significance.

I steeled my nerves. I wasn't scared to walk across

campus on my own. I'd show anyone who wanted to hurt me what my magic was capable of.

Which made this unsettling feeling in my gut... strange.

I shivered as I stepped out of my dorm hall and into the cool autumn air. I'd dressed as Red Riding Hood in a short red dress with a black corset, long black tights, and a velvet red cloak. I wasn't exactly dressed for the weather, but Luna and I would be spending most of our night indoors, partaking in the Halloween festivities on campus.

I attended Thornshire Academy, a university for witches founded hundreds of years ago when our witch ancestors migrated to the states. Here, witches learned to harness their powers for brewing potions, communing with spirits, forging wands, and casting powerful spells. All witches in Thornshire attended the academy, because learning our magic was equally a part of our religion—in which we honored our ancestors in the afterlife —as it was important to our economy. We were one of the top cranberry exporters in all of the New England area, and it was our magic that kept the bogs producing high-quality fruit at such a fast rate.

I was in my first year at the academy, but my older cousin Luna would graduate next semester. She'd promised to hand down all her campus knowledge before graduation. Tonight, she was my guide to all the best Halloween parties on campus.

Halloween was always a big to-do in Thornshire. Townspeople decorated their homes with strings of orange lights, massive lawn displays depicting giant skeletons, and oversized blow-up spiders. Businesses competed for the best window displays by enchanting cauldrons to light up and bubble or using necromancy magic to make skeletons wave at passersby. Farmers brought their biggest pumpkins to the town square, and a prize was awarded to the largest one, which always weighed over a thousand pounds. Cider tastings and hayrides were everywhere, along with ghost tours at various historical locations.

On campus, the theater department hosted a haunted house in the university's main academic building—Haunted Halls, they called it. I'd been there with Kylan a few times in high school, when we were still dating. It'd been a lot of fun, and the event only got better every year.

My heels clicked on the sidewalk as I crossed the quad toward Luna's dorm. Around me, tall Victorian structures towered several stories. Four dorm buildings that housed thousands of students faced one another to form a square, and a big lawn stretched between them. Usually, the quad was bustling with activity, but everyone must've already been at their parties, because I was alone.

I'd been running late, which Luna normally *hated*, but she'd messaged me earlier saying she was running behind as well. I checked my phone to see if she'd sent any updates, but she hadn't. It was almost ten o'clock, which was still early by witch standards, but Haunted Halls had already been open for hours. Luna and I had to get going soon or we'd miss the best festivities in the countdown to the witching hour.

As I slid my phone back into my crossbody bag, I caught sight of movement in the shadows. A breeze swept across the quad, making the hairs on the back of my neck stand straighter. I reached for my wand in my bag. If someone thought they'd pull a Halloween prank by scaring a girl like me, they could think again.

A black cat emerged from the shadows, skittering beneath the light of a streetlamp. I slowly released my grip on the wand. It was only Halloween, and I couldn't let something as simple as a black cat freak me out.

Though... a black cat crossing your path was never a good sign.

I pulled my cloak tighter around me, shooting one last glance around the quad. There was nothing there. I had to get to Luna's dorm room quickly, because she'd talk me down and convince me this was nothing to worry about.

I hurried into her dorm building. Luna's room was located on the first floor at the end of the hall. She was the resident advisor for her dorm and had one of the best rooms on campus, complete with a living room and kitchenette. She even had a fireplace she usually kept burning.

As I passed by the other rooms, my gaze locked on one door in particular. Unease twisted in my stomach, though it was entirely unrelated to the strange feeling I'd gotten outside. Kylan lived in this hall, and the last thing I wanted was to run into him. I'd seen him on the broomball field a few weeks ago when I was crossing campus. Broomball was a lot like soccer, only played on flying brooms. Kylan had been so focused on scoring a goal I didn't think he'd seen me that day, and I'd done my best to avoid him ever since.

I hurried past his room and stopped at Luna's door on the end. I knocked, but no answer came, which was weird because she was expecting me. I tried the door handle, and it twisted easily. "Luna?"

I was met only with resounding silence. When she said she was running behind, I figured she was deep in some class project like she always was and needed the extra time to get into her costume. If there was one thing that could make Luna lose track of time, it was her academics. I didn't realize she wouldn't be here when I arrived.

But then again, Luna wouldn't leave her dorm room without locking it... She must be around. She was probably just blasting haunting music in her earbuds like she did when she studied.

I called her name louder and stepped inside. An icy chill hit me, even though there were coals still glowing in the fireplace. The doors to the bedroom and the bathroom were both open, but the lights were off inside both of them. A sitting area circled the fireplace in the living room, with a long couch situated with its back facing the door.

"Very funny, Luna," I teased as I approached the sitting area. "It's not like you to fall asleep when we have plans—"

My words halted in their tracks when I caught sight of black heels pointed up toward the ceiling near the base of the couch. My heart lurched as I raced around the furniture to see Luna sprawled out across the floor. She wore a brown trench coat with a Sherlock Holmes hat askew atop her head. Her wand lay in one of her limp, outstretched hands.

"Luna!" I cried.

I dropped to my knees beside her and frantically shook her, but she remained unresponsive. Her skin appeared dull and sickly... a color I'd only seen once before. Luna remained entirely motionless, though I pleaded with our ancestors to show me the rise and fall of her chest. My prayers remained unanswered.

I pressed my fingers to the side of her throat in search of a pulse, but the all-encompassing devastation that slammed into my gut told me everything I already knew but refused to believe. This couldn't be happening again. Not to Luna.

The pulse I so desperately searched for wasn't present.

I staggered to my feet as the dread I'd felt when crossing the quad intensified into something far more sinister and horrible. The grim reaper himself might as well have curled his bony fingers around my throat, because it felt as if my terror might just rip my soul from my body right alongside Luna's. The edges of my vision blurred, and I found myself gasping for breath.

I hadn't been imagining things when I said that something bad was going to happen. Not this time. My cousin was dead, and no amount of psychic visions or cryptic warnings from beyond could save her now.

I stumbled toward the fireplace and caught myself on the mantle. For the briefest of moments, an image of flames flashed across my vision. I saw the edges of paper burning to embers, before my very real, harrowing reality came back into focus. Fingers trembling, I tore my gaze from Luna's body to peer into the fireplace.

A tiny piece of paper no larger than a quarter was

wedged in the corner, far away from the embers. I bent to inspect it. I took special care to lift the paper so that it wouldn't crumble into ashes. The edges were burnt, but I was able to make out a singular phrase typed out in small letters.

Murder in Thornshire.

Usually, my psychic abilities weren't so direct, but this vision had been unmistakable. Whatever Luna had burned earlier had been incredibly important.

And it might just be what got her killed.

Continue the story by reading Murder at the Magic Academy by Alicia Rades!

About the Authors

Megan Linski (left) and Alicia Rades (right) are best friends and USA Today Bestselling coauthors of fantasy fiction. Megan Linski is a coffee connoisseur who enjoys ice skating, horseback riding, and shopping. Her stories feature themes of community and friendship while advocating for the rights of the disabled. Alicia Rades is a mother who loves baking cookies, reading tarot, and binge-watching Netflix. She has a passion for personal development and strives to incorporate emotional-empowerment themes into her books. Both girls love nature, animals, sexy romances, and eating cheese.